Susan B. Anthony

Champion of Women's Rights

Illustrated by Al Fiorentino

Susan B. Anthony

Champion of Women's Rights

By Helen Albee Monsell

Aladdin Paperbacks

Aladdin Paperbacks
An imprint of Simon & Schuster
Children's Publishing Division
1230 Avenue of the Americas
New York, NY 10020
Copyright © 1954, 1960 by the Bobbs-Merrill Co., Inc.
All rights reserved including the right of reproduction
in whole or in part in any form
First Aladdin Paperbacks edition, 1986
Printed in the United States of America

15   14   13
Library of Congress Cataloging-in-Publication Data

Monsell, Helen Albee, 1895-
    Susan B. Anthony : champion of women's rights.

    Reprint. Originally published: Indianapolis : Bobbs-
Merrill, 1954.
    Summary: Focuses on the childhood of a pioneer in
the crusade for human rights, particularly those of
women.
    1. Anthony, Susan B. (Susan Brownell), 1820-1906—
Juvenile literature.   2. Sufragettes—United States—
Biography—Juvenile literature.   3. Feminists—United
States—Biography—Juvenile literature.   4. Women's
rights—United States—Juvenile literature.   [1. Anthony,
Susan B. (Susan Brownell), 1820-1906.   2. Feminists.
3. Women's rights]   I. Title.
HQ1413.A55M66   1986   324.6'23'0924 [B] [92] 86-10716
ISBN 0-02-041800-0

To the University of Richmond Library Staff, whose kindness in helping me has been equaled only by their uncanny skill in finding answers to the questions I asked

Illustrations

Full Pages

Numerous smaller illustrations

Contents

Books by Helen Albee Monsell

DOLLY MADISON: QUAKER GIRL

HENRY CLAY: YOUNG KENTUCKY ORATOR

JOHN MARSHALL: BOY OF YOUNG AMERICA

ROBERT E. LEE: BOY OF OLD VIRGINIA

SUSAN B. ANTHONY: CHAMPION OF WOMEN'S RIGHTS

TOM JACKSON: YOUNG STONEWALL

TOM JEFFERSON: BOY OF COLONIAL DAYS

WOODROW WILSON: BOY PRESIDENT

★ Susan B. Anthony

Champion of Women's Rights

Tinderbox and Apples

GRANDMOTHER READ's farm was in the north-western corner of Massachusetts. On a late-summer afternoon in 1825 Susan was visiting her. They were out in the garden picking beans. Grandmother reached those high up on the vines. Susan pulled the ones near the ground.

"You're a big help to me," said Grandmother. "I don't have to stoop at all."

Susan felt a pod to make sure the beans were plump. "You're a big help to me," she said. "I don't have to stretch."

Grandmother laughed. "I guess we've picked enough for supper. I'll go start the fire."

11

Susan stood up so quickly she almost dropped her basket. "Let me start it."

Grandmother looked doubtful. "It's dangerous for children to play with fire."

"This isn't play. It's work. Besides, I'll be six years old soon."

"Not until next February," said Grandmother, but she smiled. "Maybe it *is* time for you to learn. Just remember that fire is your best friend and your worst enemy. Never play with it."

They went into the kitchen. There, in the fireplace, Grandmother had laid a little pile of shavings and chips. There were bigger pieces of wood in the wood box close by. Everything was ready for the fire.

The tinderbox was on a shelf where babies couldn't reach it. When Susan stood on tiptoe her fingers could just curl around it. She pulled the box down carefully and sat on the floor to open it.

Inside was a steel wheel with a piece of cord. Susan had watched Grandmother, so she knew exactly what to do. She wound the cord around the wheel as if it were a top. Then she spun it so that it struck a hard piece of flint on the side of the box.

There was a scrap of linen in the box. It had been scorched so that it would blaze quickly. When the wheel struck a spark from the flint, Susan must catch it on the scorched linen and blow it carefully into a flame. With the flame she could light a candle. With the candle she could light the fire.

Susan was sure it would be easy. She pulled hard. Nothing happened. She pulled again. No spark! She worked until beads of water stood on her forehead. Sometimes she got a spark, but it died before she could blow it.

"You'd better let me do it," said Grandmother Read.

Susan was hurt. "Why, Grandmother! You promised I could do it. I'm going to start that fire if it takes me all night!"

Grandmother shook her head. "I don't believe your grandfather would want to wait that long for his supper." But she let Susan keep on trying a little longer.

At last a big spark flashed. It dropped just where Susan wanted it to. She blew on it—oh, so carefully. A brown spot appeared in the linen. The spot turned into a hole, with curling blue edges. Then it burst into flame.

Quickly, before the scrap of linen burned away, Susan lighted her candle. She held it under the wood shavings and chips on the fireplace until they, too, blazed. Her fire was started at last.

TIME TO GO HOME

Grandmother filled a small kettle with water from the water bucket on a side table. She hung it on a hook from the crane over the fireplace.

"Now feed your fire with bigger pieces of

wood. Be careful—not too many pieces or you will choke it. Maybe I had better do it while you finish stringing the beans."

"No, please. It's my fire."

Grandmother looked through the kitchen window at the sun. "You had better run along home instead of doing either. There is little more than an hour to sundown, and you have your own chores to do when you get home."

Susan stood up. She hated to leave her lovely fire, but Grandmother was right. She must gather her basket of wood chips from the ground around Father's chopping block. She must help feed the chickens.

"You'd better take a doughnut to eat on your way home," Grandmother said.

Susan thought that was a good idea. "It's funny," she said as she bit into the doughnut. "Between now and sundown seems like only a little while. But between now and supper is a

16

long, long while. Only we have supper at sundown, so it is really the same time."

Grandmother laughed. "Run along with you."

Susan started toward the door.

"If you cut through the orchard," Grandmother called after her, "you'll probably find
some apples that need to be eaten, too."

Grandmother was full of good ideas today.
Susan cut through the orchard. Her sister Guelma was seven years old. Her sister Hannah was
nearly four. They liked apples as well as she
did. She filled her pockets full, so that there
would be enough for them all. But the sun was
getting down near the top of old Greylock Mountain. She knew she must hurry.

Guelma and Hannah were playing in the yard
when she slipped between the fence rails. As

17

she bent over, the apples fell from her pockets. The chickens saw them and came scurrying.

Susan didn't want any chicken-pecked apples. "Shoo, now! Shoo!" she cried.

Guelma and Hannah ran to help her. They picked up the apples.

"Let's eat them now," said Hannah. "It's a long time before supper."

But Susan had already started for her chip basket. "It isn't any fun to eat apples and think about the work you still have to do," she called back. "I'd rather eat them and think about the work that is all done."

"I suppose you're right," Guelma agreed. "I'll go set the supper table first."

She put the apples on top of the fence and hurried into the kitchen. Hannah trotted along after Susan to help pick up the chips.

When the basket was full they carried it into the kitchen.

18

Susan sniffed hungrily. "Hasty pudding!" she said. "Um-m-m."

Mother smiled. "Supper will be ready in less than no time now," she told Susan. "'But go rock the cradle a bit, please. Baby's been fretful this afternoon. He doesn't want to go to sleep."

Susan stood at the head of the big cradle. She looked down at her little brother Daniel. "I believe he wants you to sing to him, Mother. Why won't you ever sing? Don't you like to?"

Mother turned from the fireplace. She brushed a wisp of hair back from her forehead with her wrist. "Do you know what I'd like to do? I'd like to go down in the middle of the two-acre lot where nobody could hear me and sing at the top of my voice."

"Then why don't you?"

"Quakers don't think it is right to sing."

"But you aren't a Quaker."

"Your father is."

"Do you *have* to do things his way?"

"I *want* to do things his way."

"But suppose you didn't want to?"

Mother shook her head. "Too many questions from too little a girl. There! Daniel has dropped off to sleep at last. And Guelma has finished setting the table. Clear out from under foot, now, until I call."

The three girls skipped outdoors. They ran to the fence for their apples. Then they sat on the well curb to eat. For a few minutes they were too busy to talk, but Susan was still thinking.

Finally, between mouthfuls, she asked, "Suppose Mother didn't want to do things Father's way?"

"She'd have to anyway," Guelma replied.

"Why?"

"Wives always have to do what their husbands say."

"That's not fair."

"It's the law."

"Then somebody ought to change the law."

"Don't talk nonsense." Guelma threw her apple core to the chickens and stood up. "Come on. Let's play tag."

Sharing

THE NEXT morning was a busy one. Not only was it baking day, but Mother was making apple butter. That meant the fire must be kept up all day. It meant someone must be stirring the apples in the big iron kettle. The children had more than their usual chores to do. They were almost as busy as Mother.

"Shucks!" said Susan. "I wanted to go to Grandmother Anthony's today. She promised to let me help make cheese."

"That isn't so much work as making apple butter, is it?" asked Hannah.

Susan thought for a minute. "I suppose it is

more work," she said honestly. "But Grandmother *lets* me help, and here I *have* to."

"Well, then," said Mother, "I'll *let* you take this pan of scraps to the chickens."

The children laughed. Susan hurried out with the pan of scraps. Little Hannah followed at her heels.

Susan liked the outdoor chores. She was sorry that Hannah was almost big enough now to pick up chips and help Mother gather the eggs. That meant that Susan must start taking on Guelma's indoor chores—setting the table and making the beds. Guelma would begin to help Mother with the cooking and sewing.

Cooking wasn't bad. Susan was pretty sure that she would like cooking. But sewing! Sitting still, pricking your fingers! And Mother saying, "No, dear, that is crooked. Pull it out and do it again." Just thinking of the little sewing she had done made her impatient.

"I hate sewing!" Susan said. "I wish nobody had ever heard of it." Suddenly she thought of something else. "But then I'd never have a new dress."

She thought of her new dress hanging on a peg upstairs. Of course it was plain. A Quaker's children wore plain clothes. But Mother knew how to make a plain dress pretty, even without ruffles. Susan loved her new dress. While it was still new, though, she could wear it only to meeting on First Day. She did wish she could wear it every day in the week and not just on Sunday.

"That small chicken isn't getting anything," said Hannah. "The others gobble it all first."

Susan threw the last scrap to the small chicken.

GRANDMOTHER ANTHONY IS PLEASED

"My, but the apple butter smells good!" Grandmother Anthony stood in the doorway.

The children ran to her. Somehow she managed to hug all of them at once. She felt in her big pocket and pulled out a package. "I cut a few pieces of maple sugar from the tub as I came by."

Even little Hannah remembered to say "Thank you" without being reminded.

"Now shoo along outside, children," Grandmother said, "while I talk with thy mother."

"Do sit down, Mother Anthony," Mother told her. "Susan, pull a chair near the door before you go out, so that Grandmother may catch the breeze."

"I can't stay more than a minute or two, but thee might as well hand over that pan of apples and a knife. I can work while I talk."

The children went outside. They sat down on the doorstep like three little birds on the branch of a tree.

Susan bit into her cake of hard sugar. "I feel

sorry for children who don't have grandmothers," she said.

"We're lucky," Guelma agreed. "Grandmother and Grandfather Read live just on the other side of the orchard. Grandmother and Grandfather Anthony live right up the hill behind us. We have Father, Mother, two grandmothers and two grandfathers. Not many children have all of them still living."

Grandmother Anthony heard her. "The child is right," she told Mother. "That is why I have come. The Smith children's mother died last night."

"Oh!" Susan caught her breath. Suppose it had been *her* mother! She tried to think how life would be without Mother. Poor, poor little Smith children!"

Grandmother was still talking. "All the long time Mrs. Smith was ill she couldn't do anything for her family. Really, the girls haven't a stitch that is fit to wear. The neighbors will help as best they can. By cold weather I think we can have a nice, warm outfit for each child. But right now, while everyone is busy canning——"

Susan jumped up from the doorstep and hurried in. "Mother! Can't I lend Prudence Smith my dress until the neighbors make hers? I have my new one, you know."

Grandmother Anthony smiled. "Thee is a good child, Susan."

Mother thought aloud. "It might be a good idea."

Grandmother stood up. "I must hurry back home now to fix dinner. But if thee will have the dress ready when I go down there this afternoon——"

"I'll send some eggs, too," Mother said, "and a new loaf of rye bread. Susan can help you carry them."

Grandmother Anthony gave Susan a little pat

27

as she went out. "Thee is a good child," she said again.

Susan thought so, herself. It made her feel warm inside to know that she was helping Prudence Smith. Besides, while Prudence was wearing the old dress, Mother would have to let Susan wear the new one—every day! How fresh and fine she would look!"

"Guelma and I are going to lend our dresses, too," said Hannah.

Susan hardly heard her. She was too busy thinking about her new frock.

TURNABOUT

Soon after Grandmother Anthony left, Mother came to the door. "You may ring the bell, children."

The girls raced to the great outdoor bell. They pulled hard on the long rope. *Ding dong!*

Mother had fixed a boiled dinner. There was a big piece of beef on the pewter platter, with cabbage, beets and carrots heaped all around. For a while everyone was too busy eating to talk.

After dinner Father rested a few minutes before going back to the mill. Mother told him then about Mrs. Smith and how his daughters were going to lend their dresses. Father was pleased, too. "A child is never too young to share with others," he said.

As soon as he left, Mother turned briskly to her work. "Now we'll get the basket ready for Grandmother Anthony. I have a few more stitches to take in Guelma's new dress. Susan, you go get yours———"

Susan was stunned. "My *new* dress?"

"Of course. You wouldn't want to lend your old one, would you?"

Susan certainly did want to lend her old one. It was quite good enough for a girl who didn't have anything. If Prudence wore her new one, it wouldn't be new any more when she got it back.

"Come, come!" said Mother. "Don't just stand there. Go get your dress."

Susan went slowly up the stairs. She went into the room where she and her two sisters slept and took her new dress down from its peg. She ran her hand softly over its smooth, unwrinkled skirt.

"Susan!" Mother called.

"I'm coming," said Susan.

She knew that "the Lord loveth a cheerful giver." She supposed He loved a cheerful lender, too. But she didn't feel the least bit cheerful as she carried the dress downstairs.

After she started off with Grandmother, though, Susan felt better. The sky was blue, with white clouds drifting by. There was a good breeze blowing. She couldn't stay glum on a day like this. She picked a handful of sour grass and nibbled it slowly.

After all, her old dress was comfortable. And she wouldn't be so worried about getting it spotted or torn. If she had on her new dress, she wouldn't dare to jump the brook that ran by the side of the road.

"Look, Grandmother! Hold my basket a minute, please. See how far I can jump!" With a run and a leap Susan was across the little brook. Then with another jump she was back.

"Fine!" said Grandmother. "I hope thy mind will be equally nimble when thee starts to school."

"Oh!" said Susan. "The book part of school is easy. It's the sitting still I'm going to hate. Grandmother, will you ask Mother if I can come help you make cheese tomorrow?"

Making Cheese

GRANDFATHER had finished milking, but the morning was still dewy wet when Susan started up to Grandmother Anthony's house. The mountains were dim in the mist. Even the pine trees were a blurred, blue-green mass.

Grandmother was standing in the kitchen doorway, pouring the morning's milk from one big pan to another. She held it high, so that the fresh morning air would cool it as she poured.

"Thee is just in time," she told Susan. "Go put the rennet in the big dipper. Thee can measure it thyself. Two tablespoonfuls will be about enough to curdle the milk."

33

Susan knew that rennet was what Grandmother added to the milk to make the curd come. She knew where it was—on the shelf in the room off the kitchen. All the things for making cheese were kept there. She pulled down the rennet jar

from the shelf and took the big dipper from its nail. She filled the big dipper half full of water and dissolved the rennet.

By that time Grandmother had poured the milk into a large shallow vat. "Now, add the rennet, Susan," she said.

Susan stirred the rennet into the milk.

"Good! Now we'll cover it up and go wash the breakfast dishes."

Susan couldn't keep her mind on the dishes. "Don't you suppose it's ready by now?" she kept asking.

Grandmother laughed. "Give it time, child." But at last she said, "Go peep if thee wants."

Susan lifted a corner of the cloth which covered the shallow vat. "The milk is all curdled," she called. "Honestly it is. Come see!"

Grandmother pushed her finger under the curd and lifted it carefully. "It isn't thick enough yet. Come back and finish the dishes."

"I hate to wait," Susan fretted. "I like to do everything quick. Like that!" She flicked her towel to show how quickly things should be done.

The towel hit a mug of milk on the table and knocked it to the floor with a bang. The mug was pewter. It couldn't break. But the milk splashed everywhere.

Grandmother didn't stop to scold. She caught up a cloth. "Here! Mop it up."

Susan mopped until the floor was dry. Then she looked up. "Maybe," she admitted, "not everything has to be done *that* quick."

Grandmother smiled. "Thee learns, my child. Thee is impatient sometimes, but thee learns. Now, let's look at the curd again."

Susan couldn't see that it looked very different. But this time when Grandmother tried to raise it on her finger, it broke—a clean break, with no flakes. The curd was ready.

"That is better. Thee can get the knives now."

Susan brought several knives, which were fastened together somewhat like wires in an egg beater. Grandmother let her draw the knives through the thick curd until it was cut into pieces no bigger than kernels of corn.

After that the cheese in the vat was heated very slowly. Then they drew off the whey. They put cheesecloth in the mold.

At last everything was ready. With big, double handfuls, Susan heaped the curd into the mold until it was full. Grandmother covered it, turned it, and put it in the cheese press.

"There!" said Susan happily. "It's done."

"Done!" cried Grandmother. "Why, it is only begun. This afternoon we must press it. Then we must press it again for at least twenty hours. After that we'll put it on the shelf in the cheese house. But we'll still have to turn it every day for a month. Then we'll turn it once a week."

That didn't suit Susan at all. "I wanted to take a slice home today to show Guelma and Hannah what fine cheese I can make."

"Tch, tch. It is just as well thee can't. Doesn't thee know it is a sinful thing to be puffed up with pride?"

"I don't see why it's wrong to be proud of something that is worth being proud of."

"Thy pleasure should come from a task well done—not from showing it off to others."

Susan thought this over. "I do have a nice feeling inside me when I've done something just right," she admitted. "And I like secrets, too. Maybe you're right. If I keep the nice feeling a secret——"

GRANDFATHER LIKES CHEESE

"Who is having a secret about what?" Grandfather Anthony came into the kitchen.

"Secrets," Grandmother Anthony said quickly, "aren't for telling."

"I suppose not. But cheeses are made for eating. How about cutting me a piece?"

"Oh, no!" cried Susan. "You can't have it for weeks and weeks. Can he, Grandmother?"

"Thy grandfather is just teasing. He knows no cheese is fit to eat until it is at least three months old. Draw him a dipper of the whey, Susan. It is a cooling drink for a hot day."

Grandfather drank deeply. "I like cheese," he said. "I like whey. It is a good thing I married the best cheese-maker in the county. I do believe, Susan, that if thy grandmother had made it, I could have eaten every crumb of the Cheshire Cheese."

"What is the Cheshire Cheese?"

"Ask thy grandmother. I must get back to the field."

"Please let me ride with you."

Susan loved to ride over the rocky lane in Grandfather's hay wagon. It was so bumpy that if she held her mouth just right it would make her teeth rattle.

But Grandmother had other ideas. She sat down in her chair by the window and reached for her knitting. "Come hold my yarn for me, child, while I wind a fresh ball."

Susan pouted. When Grandmother wound yarn Susan had to stand like a stone statue with her arms stretched out stiff in front of her, holding the skein. If her nose itched or if a fly buzzed around her head, she couldn't do a thing. She just had to stand there. It wasn't right for Grandmother to make her do it today. She ought to let her have a good time.

But then Susan's face cleared. Maybe she could get a good story out of it. Grandmother could tell very good stories.

She stood in front of Grandmother and held

out her arms. Grandmother slipped the skein of wool over them. "Stand still, now. Don't fidget."

"I'll try not to. But maybe it would be easier if you told me a story while we're working."

Grandmother laughed. "All right. What story would you like to hear?"

THE CHESHIRE CHEESE

"Tell me about the Cheshire Cheese," said Susan. "Who made it?"

"The farmers of Cheshire—right here in our own state of Massachusetts."

"How big was the cheese?"

"It weighed over a half ton."

Susan nearly dropped the yarn. "A half ton! I don't see how anybody could have had enough milk to make a cheese that big."

"No one person did. But when a lot of people

work together they can do ever so many things that no one of them could do by himself.

"The people of Cheshire wanted to send a present to Thomas Jefferson when he became President of the United States. None of them was rich. All of them were farmers, though, and each one could spare a morning's milk.

"'Bring it to Farmer Brown's farm next Thursday,' each was told.

"All morning long farmers' carts rattled up to Farmer Brown's with their big cans of milk. Mr. Brown and his helpers had a busy time of it, making curd."

Susan remembered how long she and Grandmother had worked over just one vat of milk. "I guess they did," she said.

"When the cheese was ready," Grandmother went on, "it took six oxen to draw the wagon that carried it to the boat on which it was shipped to Washington."

"Did President Jefferson like it?"

"He surely did. He gave some to everyone in the White House—the visitors, the servants, everybody. He sent back a big slice for each farmer and each farmer's wife who had helped make it. And six months later there was still some left!"

A neat ball had been made of Grandmother's yarn now. She wound the last loop from Susan's hands. "There! That is done. Now thee can run up to the field and ride back with thy grandfather."

Winter Days

Susan knew that Grandfather Anthony was hurrying to get his crops in before the first frost. Summer couldn't last forever. The first gray, cold autumn days weren't exactly a surprise, but she didn't like them.

"I'd forgotten how mean and uncomfortable weather could be," she grumbled to herself early one morning.

But it was cozy and warm under the blankets. With a little twist she snuggled down deep in the bed.

"Girls, girls!" Mother called. "Time to get up! Time to get up!"

"Guelma's oldest," Susan thought. "I'll make her get up first."

Guelma rolled over sleepily. Then she sat up. She pulled the blankets with her so that cold air came rushing down into Susan's warm nest. Susan quickly decided she should get up, too. But doing something she didn't want to do always made her feel a little unhappy.

This was the first week she had worn her winter underthings. They were still stiff and scratchy.

The water in the washstand pitcher was so cold it pricked like needles. "It might just as well be frozen," Susan complained to Guelma.

"More than likely it will be in a few days," Guelma declared cheerfully. "There was probably a stiff frost last night."

"It is too cold to dress up here, anyway—that is certain." Susan caught up the rest of her clothes and hurried down to the kitchen fire.

The kitchen was a busy place in the early morning. As soon as breakfast was over, Susan started clearing the table. Guelma went upstairs to make the beds. Mother started out to feed the chickens.

When Mother came back she was shivering. "The wind seemed to go right through me. And it's so gloomy out. You children will have to play inside today."

Susan didn't want to play inside. "Whenever we begin having a really good time you always ask us not to make such a fuss."

"Sometimes your games are rather noisy," Mother said with a laugh. "Why don't you get your sewing and sit in the chimney corner where it is warm?"

Susan shook her head. She had been very eager to learn to sew because she always wanted to do whatever Guelma was doing. But Guelma was making a sampler now, and Mother said

Susan was too young to start a sampler. She must learn first to stitch a long, even hem. Susan hated making long, even hems, but she didn't want to admit it. "Hannah's too little to sew," she said instead. "We ought to do something she would like, too."

"Play bear?" Hannah suggested.

"All right. Let's," Susan agreed.

"Not too noisy now," Mother warned.

"Bears have to growl a little bit," Susan said, "but we'll play baby bear."

BEAR AND BABY BEAR

Guelma had finished her upstairs work now. She was ready to play, too. They put two chairs back to back, far enough apart for a bear to creep between them. Then they fastened Mother's big shawl over the chair backs to make a den. Underneath the shawl it was dark and scary.

48

"I'm the oldest," Guelma said. "I'll be bear first."

"No," Hannah said. "Me first. I'm youngest."

It would be silly to say "It's my first turn because I am the middle one." So Susan suggested, "Let's count out."

That was fair. Guelma began to count. But this wasn't Susan's lucky day. The count gave Hannah first turn. Happily she crawled into the den.

"Now, when we come close, you must jump out and grab us," Guelma told her. "The last one caught can be bear the next time."

Hannah let one end of the shawl drop over the mouth of the cave. Guelma and Susan crouched under the window.

"Gr-r-r!" growled Hannah, the baby bear.

"Gr-r-r!" came a growl from the doorway. It wasn't any baby-bear growl. It was deep and fierce. A gust of cold air blew through the room.

49

Susan and Guelma were so startled they nearly knocked each other over. Had a real bear come down from the mountains?

Then the growl changed to a jolly laugh. The children looked up. Grandfather Anthony was standing in the doorway, laughing at them.

The children ran across the room. They threw their arms around him.

"Gr-r-r, yourself!" Susan laughed. "Come over to the fireplace and get warm."

"I just stopped to bring thy father the axhead he wanted," Grandfather told her. Then he turned to Mother. "I'm on my way to the wood lot. Will thee let the children ride halfway up with me? I will let them off near the hickory trees. They can gather nuts. And when they get tired they can run on down to their grandmother's."

Mother shook her head. "It looks as if it might rain or snow any minute."

"What if it does? The girls are neither sugar nor salt. They won't melt."

Still Mother looked doubtful.

"After the first frost but before the first snow —that is the best time to go nutting," Grandfather added with a twinkle in his eyes.

"Please, Mother," cried Susan and Guelma together.

"Well-l——"

The girls ran for their hoods and coats before she could say no. Susan bundled Hannah into her coat while Guelma got the pails for their nuts.

Then they were outdoors, climbing into the back of Grandfather's wagon.

Lost in the Woods

"HOLD TIGHT!" Grandfather said. They were off, up the hillside road. It was filled with rocks and deep ruts. The wagon jolted until the children had to hold to the sides and to one another to keep from falling out.

"It's f-f-fun!" Susan called to Grandfather on the seat in front. The bumps jolted the words from her mouth.

"It's f-fun," repeated little Hannah.

When they reached the clump of hickory trees, Grandfather stopped to let them climb down.

"Don't wait for me to go back," he said. "Just run along down to thy grandmother's."

The frost had opened the thick hulls of the hickory nuts. Nuts lay deep in the dead leaves. It was fun to scuff through the leaves to find them. But the squirrels had found a good many of them first. Nut after nut that Susan picked up showed where the squirrels' sharp teeth had bored deep for the food inside.

Susan began to feel a little cross. The wind was finding its way inside her thick wool scarf. Her fingers, even though she was wearing mittens, ached with cold.

"Every time I find a good place," she told Guelma, "you come pick under the same tree."

"Why shouldn't I?" Guelma asked. "They're my nuts as much as they are yours."

Susan had to admit that Guelma was right. But she didn't want Guelma to get ahead of her. So she decided to look harder than ever.

"I'm going over to that big tree by myself," she said. "It looks like a good place."

"Go ahead. I'll stay here."

When Susan reached the tree by the big rock, she found that the squirrels had been ahead of her again. Only a few good nuts were left.

She went farther on—and on—and on. Hannah, who wanted to go, too, kept close to her. But Guelma stayed on the other side of the rock.

Susan didn't know how far she had gone into the woods when something white fluttered down and hit her on the nose. She looked up, startled. Snow!

"Goodness!" she told Hannah. "We'd better be getting back." But which way was back? Frightened, she looked around. She didn't know.

Hannah could tell that Susan was afraid. Soon she became frightened, too, and began to cry. "I want to go home! We're lost!" Hannah wailed.

"Don't cry," Susan told her, trying to be brave. "I'll take you home."

But the trees all looked exactly alike. The snow drifting down made everything blurry white. Susan felt as small and lost as Hannah.

"Guelma!" she called. "Guelma!"

There was no answer.

"Guelma!" she called again. She went first one way, then another. "Guelma! Guelma!"

At last there came a faint answer. She called again. Finally, through the snow, Guelma came toward them.

"I hunted and hunted for you," Guelma said. "What made you go so deep into the woods?"

"We got lost," Hannah told her.

"That's right." Susan was ashamed but honest. "Which way should we go, Guelma?"

Guelma looked around. Hunting for her sisters, she had become confused, too. "I just don't know," she admitted.

"We're still lost," said Hannah. She looked ready to cry again.

But with Guelma there Susan was no longer afraid. "Nonsense! Guelma and I can find the way."

"Of course," said Guelma bravely. "Even if

we can't find the road we know that home is downhill."

"And as soon as we find the brook," Susan added, "we can follow that."

With Hannah between them, they started down the hill. The leaves made scrunchy sounds beneath their feet. Sometimes the bare briers caught at their legs and held them back.

Finally the three girls came to the brook. There was only a trickle of water, but it showed them the way. Soon they could see more sky through the trees. Then suddenly they found themselves out of the woods, on the hillside just above Grandmother Anthony's house. They weren't lost any more!

APPLE TOAST

"Well now," Grandmother Anthony said, "it's nipping cold outside, isn't it? Hang thy things on the peg by the door and come sit near the fire and toast thy toes."

She took Hannah in her lap and rubbed her cold hands, while Guelma and Susan brought stools close to the fire. Its warm glow soon thawed them out.

Now that she could forget her hands and feet, Susan began to feel another ache. It had been a long, long time since breakfast. She looked about the room. Suddenly her eyes grew wide. She saw the porringers or small pewter bowls which hung in a row from a shelf.

"Grandmother! Let's make apple toast. Please!"

"That's not such a bad notion on a cold day like this. Go get a loaf of rye bread from the buttery. And thee can get the toasting fork, Guelma, from the drawer in the kitchen table."

When Susan came back with a round loaf of rye bread, Guelma had the long fork ready. "Who gets first go at toasting?" she asked. "Shall we count out?"

"We'll let you have first go," said Susan, "because you found us when we were lost. I'll go get the porringers."

Guelma toasted the outside of the rye loaf to a fine even brown. She peeled this crust off carefully. Then, while she broke it into small pieces in the porringers, it was Susan's turn to toast. The loaf grew smaller each time they peeled off the crust. It took less and less time to toast the next round.

"We have almost enough," said Guelma. "I had first turn—you can have last." She handed Susan the bread and the toasting fork.

Hannah had fallen asleep in Grandmother's arms. Grandmother took her into the bedroom off the kitchen and covered her with a warm blanket. Then she went to the buttery again and came back with a mug of apple juice. She added hot water from the kettle over the fire and poured it over the toasted crusts.

"Um-m-m," said Guelma as she took her first bite.

"Um-m-m," agreed Susan.

Something Happens

Winter came early in northwestern Massachusetts that year. And it stayed late. Father said it was a hard winter, but Susan didn't think so at all. There were snowmen to be built and snowballs to be thrown. There were rides on the big sled behind the oxen with Grandfather Anthony.

Susan's birthday came on February 15. It was good to be six years old. Grandmother Read gave her a sampler for a birthday present. It was to be worked with soft, bright-colored woolen threads. When she and Guelma sat sewing their samplers, Susan felt almost as old as her sister.

Her stitches were just as tiny and regular as Guelma's. Mother said so. Susan had learned to like this kind of sewing.

Even though she enjoyed the winter, Susan didn't want it to last forever. By springtime she had become restless.

"I want something to happen," she told Guelma one bright April morning.

"What?"

"I don't know exactly, but something exciting."

"Maybe Father will take you to Adams the next time he goes."

"I want to go farther than just to Adams. I want to go and go and go——"

"Why, Susan?" asked Hannah, who entered the room. "What's wrong with home?"

"Nothing is wrong with home, and I don't know exactly why I want to go and go and go. I just do, I guess," answered Susan.

"Look," interrupted Guelma. She pointed out the window. "Who is that man coming up the road? Do you recognize him?"

Susan turned to look out the window. "Why, I believe it's Judge McLean," she said.

"The Judge is one of Father's friends. He often stops to see Father when he comes to Massachusetts on business."

"I wonder whether he's coming to see Father again," said Guelma. "He certainly has been here a lot this winter. Why, it has been only a few weeks since he was here last."

"I like the Judge," Hannah said. "He's very friendly. Don't you think so, Susan?"

Susan didn't answer. She had already gone back to her daydreams. "I know where I'd like to go," she said. "I want to go as far away as where Judge McLean comes from."

"Why, Susan, that's over in New York State," Guelma said. "That's a long way from here."

"Um-hum," Susan answered. "I know it, but I want to go to New York State."

Guelma laughed. "You're just silly, Susan," she said. "It's ever so much nicer here at home, isn't it, Hannah?"

Hannah hesitated. It always worried her to have to choose between her big sisters. "Well, I don't know," she said finally. "Home is nice and New York may be nice, too."

"That's right," Susan agreed, laughing. "Both of them are nice."

"H'm," said Guelma. "What you want, then, is to live in New York State."

The idea was so ridiculous that they all broke out laughing.

They were still giggling when Judge McLean rode into the yard and got down from his horse. He walked toward the house. The girls went to the door to meet him.

"Is your father here?" he asked.

The girls stopped laughing. They made their little curtseys to him very primly.

"We're not sure whether Father is home or not," said Guelma, "but won't you please come in while we call Mother?"

They took the Judge to the parlor and Guelma went to find Mother.

Susan wondered whether she should be polite and talk to the Judge or keep quiet.

While she was trying to decide, Hannah said, "Is New York State a good place to live?"

"Why, yes," said Judge McLean. "Why?"

"Susan wants to live there."

"She does?" exclaimed the Judge. "That's very interesting." He turned to Susan. "You must tell your father that, my dear."

Just then Mother and Guelma came in and the girls were free to slip away.

Susan told Guelma what the Judge had said. "Why did he want me to tell Father?"

"I don't know," said Guelma. "It's hard to tell what grown people mean sometimes."

Susan wanted to ask Father what the Judge had meant, but she didn't have a chance. After supper Father lighted his lantern.

"Where is he going?" asked Susan.

"He's going to see Grandfather Anthony so they can talk things over."

"What things?"

"Little girls shouldn't ask questions," said Mother, but Susan could tell that Mother was worried about something.

Susan didn't like for Mother to be worried. She couldn't sleep when she went to bed, and was still awake when Father came in. She heard him and Mother go to their bedroom.

Then she could hear them talking. "Whatever in the world?" she wondered. When she fell asleep at last they were still talking.

EXCITING NEWS

The next morning everything started off as briskly as usual. After breakfast Father said to Mother, "Shall I speak now?"

68

And Mother said, "Now is as good a time as any. Sit down, children. Father has something to tell you."

It seemed strange for all of them to be sitting down in the kitchen on a workday morning. It felt almost as quiet and serious as if they were in meeting.

"Judge McLean came to see me yesterday," said Father.

The children nodded.

"And he said for Susan to tell you she wanted to live in New York," Hannah remembered.

"She does?" Father was surprised.

"I didn't mean it," Susan explained. "It was just a sort of joke."

"I hope you do mean it, because that is where you are going to live," Father went on. "Judge McLean is building a big cotton mill at Battenville, over in New York State. He wants me to run it for him."

"We have a mill here," Susan pointed out.

"Not half so big as the new one," Father said. "And there will be a store where the millworkers can buy everything they need. We must build homes for them, too."

Susan felt prickles of excitement going down her back. "Do we start tomorrow?" she asked.

"Good lands, no!" Mother cried. "We can't get ready that soon."

Susan felt relieved. It is one thing to want to go and go and go, and another to find suddenly that you *have* to do it.

"I'm glad we don't have to tell everybody good-by today," she said soberly.

"How far is it to Battenville?" asked Hannah.

"Nearly fifty miles," Father answered.

Susan began to feel the excited prickles again. Not a boy or girl she knew had ever traveled fifty miles.

Mother stood up. "And now we had better

all be getting back to our work. Will you bring me the egg basket, Susan?"

Susan didn't hear Mother speak. She was wondering what she would find in New York State.

"Susan!" Mother called again, as she disappeared through the kitchen doorway.

"Oh! Yes, Mother, I'm coming," Susan said in a faraway voice.

"Here, take the basket," laughed Guelma. Then she wrapped Susan's fingers about the handle of the big brown egg basket.

Off to New York

DURING THE next three months Susan was never sure whether she was happy or unhappy. Part of the time she could hardly wait to start moving. Part of the time she didn't think she could stand telling everybody and everything good-by. She'd miss Grandfather and Grandmother Read, Grandfather and Grandmother Anthony, the little brook, the spring up in the pasture, and Greylock Mountain behind their home.

But no matter which way she felt, the time for leaving drew nearer and nearer. Father had gone ahead to Battenville to help Judge McLean get the mill started. Mother began to take up carpets and pack big chests with blankets and linen. At last even the beds were taken apart. The furniture was loaded in the farm wagon and started on its way. Mother and the children spent their last night at Grandmother Read's.

In the early morning Judge McLean's two fine horses pulled his big green wagon up to the house. His grandson Aaron jumped down to help the Anthonys in—first Mother with little Daniel, then Guelma. Then—"Up you go!"— he lifted Susan over the wheel. Hannah was soon nestled in her usual place between her two sisters.

The whip cracked. The wheels began to roll. Good-by! Good-by! They were off.

For a long time the way seemed homey and familiar. Their own little river ran along by the side of the road. At noon they stopped to rest both themselves and the horses. They ate dinner which Mother had prepared for them.

In the afternoon their river was left behind. Susan didn't know just when they crossed from Massachusetts into New York. By that time she was tired and sleepy. She was sore from the jolting and jouncing of the wagon. Sometimes Aaron would help her down from the wagon. Then she could run along by the horses long enough to get the stiffness out of her legs.

But it didn't help much. The day was hot and sticky. Soon she was glad to climb back into the wagon again.

Somewhere they stopped to rest the horses once more. Or maybe they changed them. Susan wasn't sure. She was nearly asleep.

Sunset came and then darkness. Still they kept on and on and on. At last Susan felt Mother shaking her shoulder.

"Wake up, Susan! Wake up!"

The horses were plodding up a hill. Ahead, lights were twinkling through the darkness. She could hear water close by, bubbling and swishing as it tumbled over rocks.

"Hello! Hello!" shouted Aaron.

Then the horses stopped. She could see a big house by the side of the road. A door opened. There were candles burning in the hallway.

"Wake up, Susan," Mother said again. "We have reached our journey's end."

Susan stood up. "But this can't be our house," she said sleepily. "Someone else is living in it. Look, there is Mrs. McLean standing in a doorway."

Aaron grinned. "It is Grandfather McLean's house," he told her. "But it's big enough for two families. Grandfather is going to rent half of it to your father until he has time to build a home of his own."

"Oh!" Susan said.

"First, though, you'll all visit with Grandmother in her side of the house for a day or two.

That will give your mother time to get things settled over on your side."

As he helped Susan jump down from the wagon, Aaron told her more. "Everyone will eat together at a long, long table. Grandmother McLean will use her best linen and dishes, because you are our company. You'll sleep in the big wooden bed that Grandfather made himself."

"Oh!" said Susan again. She was too sleepy to care on which side of the house she slept. All she wanted was a nice, cool bed.

First Day

WHEN Susan awoke the next morning she couldn't think for a moment where she was. The bed was strange. So were the pictures on the wall. So were the trees outside the window. Was she dreaming?

Just then Guelma wakened. She looked puzzled, too. Somewhere outside a rooster crowed. There came a boy's whistle.

Then suddenly Susan remembered. "We're in the McLean home at Battenville," she said.

"Yes," Guelma answered. "That must be Aaron whistling. He's probably driving his grandmother's cow out to pasture."

"Come on," said Susan, jumping out of bed. "I want to see what outdoors looks like."

Guelma was as eager as her sister. They had never dressed more quickly. But when they reached the hall, breakfast smells were coming up the steep stairs.

Susan sniffed. "Fried ham and pancakes!"

Guelma sniffed also. "And it might be hasty pudding, too. I wouldn't be surprised if Mrs. McLean is fixing company breakfast."

"Maybe," Susan decided, "we'd better not go out just yet. We'll go as soon as breakfast is over."

After breakfast, though, Mother had other ideas. "We'll go over to the rooms on our side of the house and start getting things unpacked and settled right away."

"It doesn't make any difference where we live," Susan grumbled to Guelma. "It's always work, work, work."

But even when she grumbled Susan never did anything halfway. Mother herself couldn't have dusted or rubbed or scrubbed any harder than she did. Susan was pleased to see the big kitchen lose its empty look. They unpacked their pots and pans and hung them over the fireplace. They unrolled their rag rugs. They brought in their tables and chairs.

"Why," said Susan, "it looks like home already!"

Mother was pleased. "I think so, too. Now, let's start on the upstairs."

LOOKING AROUND

By afternoon the girls' work was finished. "You still have an hour or two before supper," Mother told them. "You can run along now and see if you like it outside as well as you do in."

They stepped through a side door into a little

yard. Hannah was still too small to be much help with the work. She had been out there playing for some time. Another girl was with her.

"This is Abigail," Hannah told her sisters. "Everybody calls her Abby. She's six years old —just like Susan. She lives in the white house up the street."

Abby looked at them shyly.

Susan felt shy, too. She hadn't met new girls very often.

"We're making dandelion chains," Hannah said. "You can make some if you want to."

"Not now," Guelma told her. "We want to look around."

Abby stood up, spilling the dandelions from her lap. "I'll go with you," she said. "I can show you things."

Hannah jumped up, too. "I'm coming along."

They followed a path around the side of the house to the street in front.

"Battenville certainly is on the side of a hill," said Susan. "The road goes up. The road goes down. Doesn't it ever go straight along?"

Abby shook her head. "The river doesn't either. Can't you hear it rushing over the stones?"

They could indeed.

"That must be where the mill is," said Susan. "Let's go there."

It was only a short way to the big open gates which led to the new mill. Susan had never seen such a long, large building before. "Goodness!" she cried. "It makes the old one back home look like a baby. It doesn't seem as if there could be enough cotton in the world to keep it busy."

"And where will Father ever find enough girls to work in it?" Guelma asked.

"You don't need to worry about that," Abby said. "He'll find more than he can hire. It's much easier for a girl to work twelve hours a day in the mills than to do all the cooking and cleaning and weaving she'd have to do at home. Then, too, she wouldn't be paid a cent at home, and your father will give her a dollar and a half a week besides her board."

Susan thought how wonderful it would be to have a dollar and a half all her own. She had never had more than a halfpenny piece, and not even that very often. "I'd like to work in the mills," she said.

"Nonsense! What would you buy if you had a dollar and a half all your own?" Abby asked.

Then they all began to talk at once. But before they could make up their minds Hannah interrupted. "Look—coming up the hill!"

They all looked. Up the steep road came three great wagons drawn by oxen even bigger than Grandfather Anthony's. The wagons were heavily loaded. The oxen moved very slowly.

The girls forgot all about what they would buy. "They are the things for Father's store," Susan shouted. "Let's go watch them unload."

They rushed down to the new brick store where Father and Judge McLean stood waiting for the wagons.

Long Division

School was nearly over for the summer when the Anthonys arrived in Battenville. Mother decided she'd teach the children at home until the winter term began.

Susan was disappointed. Abby had told her about the good times they had at noon recess—eating lunch together and playing games.

"Not many boys come to school in summertime," Abby went on. "They're too busy on the farms. And we have a woman to teach us. We take our sewing to school."

"Don't you have the same teacher in the winter?" Susan asked in surprise.

"Goodness, no! A woman could never make the big boys behave. We have a schoolmaster then. He's cross and has a big bundle of switches. And he uses every one of them, too."

"Oh!" Susan said. "You can't scare me."

But she wasn't quite so sure about that when the time for the winter school came. Suppose she couldn't sit as still as the schoolmaster expected her to? Suppose she missed all her lessons? She was shivering as she and Guelma started for the little schoolhouse on the edge of the town.

"NO," SAID THE SCHOOLMASTER

She soon found that she needn't have worried. Only a few girls came to school during the winter term. And most of these stayed home on stormy days.

As for the few who were there, as long as

86

they kept quiet the schoolmaster paid very little
attention to them. He would set them a sentence
to copy on their slates. Once a day he would call
them before his desk to read, but most of the time
he spent teaching the boys.

Susan didn't see why she couldn't study what

the boys did. Grandmother Anthony had taught her her "a-b abs" when she was three years old. It was boring to sit and listen while the other girls worried over the first lessons in their blue-backed spellers.

" 'Oh may I not go in the way of sin,' " Abby read with much stumbling.

When Susan's turn came she would turn half-way through the book to the story of the bad boy and the farmer. " 'If good words and gentle means will not reclaim the wicked, they must be dealt with in a more severe manner,' " read Susan without a single mistake.

The boys were studying long division. Susan was sure she would like that. It sounded hard. She liked to do hard things. But Abby had been right when she said that the schoolmaster was cross and crabbed. He would use his ruler on little girls' hands as well as on little boys'. For a long time she was afraid to ask him anything.

At last she got up her courage one day when school was over. The boys had raced through the door with whoops and shouts. The girls hadn't been far behind. Susan went up to the schoolmaster's desk. She waited while he put his books away. Her heart was in her mouth.

At last he looked up. "What is it, Susan?"

Susan tried to be very, very polite. She bobbed a little curtsy. "Please, I want to learn long division with the boys."

The schoolmaster looked at her. Then he laughed. "Nonsense! What use has a girl for long division?"

"Some of the boys won't have use for it."

"That's different—they're boys."

"If they can learn it, so can I."

The schoolmaster closed his desk with a bang. "Fumadiddles!" Then, as he saw Susan's eyes fill with tears, he added more kindly, "You mustn't worry your little head about such things, my child. If a girl learns to read her Bible and count her egg money, that's all she needs to know. Run along now."

"YES," SAID SUSAN

Susan ran along. Guelma was waiting. "Hurry up, slowpoke," said Guelma. "I'll race you to the town pump. The last one there is an old cow's tail!"

Susan started to run, but her mind wasn't on the race.

Guelma won so easily she was puzzled. "What's the matter with you?" she asked.

Susan didn't answer.

Hannah asked the same thing that night when Susan, helping her to undress, forgot to take off her shoes. Again Susan didn't explain.

The next morning, when she set the table for breakfast without putting on any knives or forks,

90

Mother said firmly, "No one can think of two things at once. You must keep your mind on the task before you, Susan."

Mother was right, and that was exactly what Susan was doing. But the task before her wasn't running a race or undressing Hannah or setting the table. It was finding a way to study long division.

The next morning was cold and blustery. The wind whistled down the chimney until the fire danced.

"It will be worse at school," said Guelma, "because our wood there is green. Besides, there's a crack nearly an inch wide under the window where Susan and I sit. Br-r-r, but we're going to be cold!"

"Won't the schoolmaster let you come up to the fire long enough to get warm?" Father asked.

"Sometimes. But then we just feel colder than ever when we go back to our seats."

"Oh!" said Susan.

"What's the matter?" said Guelma.

"You just gave me an idea, that's all."

A PLAN WORKS

The girls met Abby as they started off to school.

Abby was cheerful. "It looks as if it might snow or sleet any minute. And sometimes the wind blows the sleet down the schoolroom chimney so hard it puts out the fire. Then we can all go home."

Susan didn't want that to happen today. It would spoil her plan. She looked at the fire anxiously as soon as they reached the schoolhouse. When the wind whistled down the chimney it sent spurts of smoke out over the schoolroom. But the fire didn't go out. As the boys piled on more wood it grew hotter and hotter.

Guelma had been right about the cold air coming in through the crack under the window. Susan could feel it blowing down her back. Her feet became cakes of ice. She stood it, though, until the schoolmaster called the boys to his desk for their arithmetic lesson. Then she raised her hand. "May I go to the fire?" she asked.

Nearly every little girl on the back bench had been up to the fire at least once during the morning. The schoolmaster nodded his head. He didn't notice that when Susan came up she carried her slate with her.

The schoolmaster's desk was near the fireplace. She could hear every word he said to the boys. When he gave them an example to work, she copied it on her slate. She didn't go back to her seat until the arithmetic lesson was over.

The other girls were busy filling their slates with the sentence the schoolmaster had set them to copy. Susan worked her example. She did the same thing, day after day. She learned to work harder and harder long-division problems.

FATHER IS PLEASED

The next month one of Grandmother Anthony's friends came to visit. After supper she and Mother sat by the fire sewing. The girls had their knitting. Father was mending a harness strap.

"How are the girls getting along with their schooling?" asked the old lady.

"As well as could be expected, I suppose," Mother said. "But with only one teacher and forty pupils from six to sixteen years old——"

"I can do long division," said Susan unexpectedly.

"Lands alive!" exclaimed their visitor. "A girl-child learning long division! The schoolmaster must be out of his senses."

"He doesn't know I've learned it," Susan told her honestly.

"Let's see you do an example," said Father. His tone was quiet.

Susan looked at him anxiously. Did he, too, think little girls ought not to study long division? Or did he think she was boasting?

But when she got her slate and rested it against his knee, he smiled. That meant he wasn't angry. Good!

"Do you want a long problem or a short one?" Father asked Susan, as he took the slate pencil.

"Please, a long one," answered Susan.

She worked the example he set her. It was a hard one, too. Then she worked another.

"Tch! Tch!" said the little old lady.

But Father was pleased. "When God gave you a brain, Susan, he expected you to use it."

"He didn't expect her to get puffed up about it," their guest told him.

"She isn't puffed up exactly," Father said kindly. "But it is only right for her to feel pleased when she has learned to do a hard thing well."

"H'm," said the old lady.

But Susan knew Father was right. She wasn't boastful and puffed up at all. She was only happy. Susan felt happy all over.

The House-Raising

By the next summer both the mill and the store were doing well. Susan was seven years old now. She was old enough to see that Father was still worried about something. It made her worry, too. At last she asked anxiously, "What's the matter, Father?"

The family were sitting by the doorstep after supper. Mother and the girls were knitting. Daniel could run around by himself now. He was playing in the yard.

Father always answered questions honestly. "Nothing is the matter—yet. But I am worried. Now that the mill is well started——"

"You can begin on our own home!" Susan cried.

"No. We must build houses for the millwork-ers first. The foundations are dug. The lumber is ready. The house-raising is next week."

"Then why are you worried?"

"Because men so often get to drinking at house-raisings. Then they become careless. Then they have accidents. Do you know lame Billy?"

The girls nodded.

"He went to a house-raising when he was a young man. He took a couple of drinks before he climbed up on the roof. His feet weren't quite steady. He fell, and now he's a cripple for life."

"Can't you just not have anything strong to drink?"

"It isn't so easy as that. The men demand it. Some of them won't come unless they know

99

they'll get it. Others will go home when it isn't given them. So——"

"Quick!" cried Mother. "Catch Daniel, Susan. He's chasing that cross old rooster. If it turns on him it might peck his eyes!"

Susan dropped her knitting and ran across the yard. She caught Daniel and held him tight. He didn't like that. He kicked and squirmed. And as soon as she let him go, he started after the rooster again.

"No!" cried Susan. "*No!*"

The little boy only ran faster.

"Look, Brother," Susan called. "Do you want to play horse? Sister will be your horsy. Come drive me!"

Daniel stopped. He liked to play horse. It would be more fun than chasing roosters. He caught up her apron strings for reins. "Giddyap!" he said.

Susan tossed her head as if she were a horse. She ran back across the yard with her driver racing behind her. The rooster was left alone. He flapped safely over the fence into the barnyard.

"Good for you!" Mother said when Susan dropped down on the doorstep by Father.

"I guess most children feel cross when people try to make them stop doing something," Susan told her. "I know I always do. But if you just give me something nicer to do instead——"

"That's true for grown people as well as children," Father said. "You've given me an idea, Susan. But it will be a good bit of work. Will you girls help me?"

"Of course," said all three together. "How?"

"Well, when the men come to our house-raising, they may feel dissatisfied at first. But we'll do just what you did with Daniel. We'll give them something they'll like."

"What?"

"Just suppose that every time one of them stops to rest for a minute he finds someone waiting with a pitcher of cold lemonade and a plate of gingerbread?"

"He can't help being satisfied," Mother said. "Everyone likes Mother's gingerbread."

102

"We could have doughnuts, too," said Hannah helpfully.

"I'll squeeze the lemons!" said Susan.

They were all talking at once. This was going to be fun.

LEMONADE, DOUGHNUTS AND GINGERBREAD

By eleven o'clock on the day of the house-raising Susan wasn't quite so sure about the fun. She had to be up with the sun. Even then, Mother had the fire going and a batch of doughnuts already sizzling in hot fat.

Susan rolled and squeezed lemons until her arms ached. Mother made the lemonade in big pails that were put in the springhouse to keep cool.

They piled the doughnuts and gingerbread on huge trays. All morning long, Susan and Guelma trudged up and down hill. Take down a full tray—bring back an empty one. Take down a full pail—bring back an empty one. The full pail was so heavy the two girls had to carry it between them.

Father had put planks across two sawhorses under a big oak tree. The girls rested their pails and trays there.

At first the men laughed when Susan lifted the dripping dipper from the pail and asked, "Won't you have a drink?" But they soon found out that cold lemonade was downright good on a warm summer day. They would pick up a handful of doughnuts and gingerbread and go back to work whistling. The pail would be emptied before the lemonade grew warm.

By noontime the women who were helping Mother had fixed a big dinner.

"Those men eat," Susan whispered to Guelma, "as though they had never tasted a doughnut or a piece of gingerbread in their lives."

104

After the girls ate dinner, they rested under the trees for a while.

Then the long afternoon began—trudging up and down hill again. More doughnuts! More gingerbread! More lemonade! Susan's arms ached. Her legs ached. Her back ached. Her sunbonnet had fallen off. She was sure she had a new row of freckles across her nose.

She slapped at a mosquito. "I've never seen such a long, long day in all my life," she told Guelma.

Guelma brushed back her hair from her forehead with a damp arm. "I don't believe it is ever going to end."

But it did. At last the men began to gather up their tools. Some climbed into wagons. Some who lived close by lifted their toolboxes to their shoulders to walk the short distance home. They waved good-by to the girls under the oak tree. Susan was almost too tired to wave back.

106

There were enough dinner leftovers to make a good supper, but Susan was almost too tired to eat.

"It has been a good day, though," she said.

"It has, indeed," Father agreed. "The men were satisfied. They worked hard. And there wasn't an accident."

"Now off to bed with you," Mother told the girls.

Susan was quite ready to go. But it was good to feel tired and happy at the same time.

She slipped into her nightgown and lay drowsily on her bed, looking through the window at the stars. Yonder was the Big Dipper. She wondered if the Great Bear drank lemonade from it. Maybe it rained when he spilled some of it. Maybe—— With a contented little squirm she was sound asleep.

Snowstorm

AFTER such a good beginning, the houses for the millworkers were soon finished. Father, though, was still too busy to build a new home for his own family. Instead, soon after the house-raising, he moved them to a house not far from Judge McLean's.

It was good to have a whole house to themselves again, even though it meant more rooms to be kept clean. But almost four years had passed since they moved to Battenville, and now Susan could sweep and dust almost as well as Guelma.

Sometimes, she decided, it was quite puzzling

to be eleven years old. There were days when she felt as if she were still a little girl. There were other days when she felt almost grown. Which was she? She just didn't know.

Mother still set her a daily stint of knitting, but it was a good long stint. And she had already pieced a whole quilt by herself. Still she would rather climb trees with her brother Daniel than sit by the fireside with her workbasket.

This week, she knew, the big-girl feeling should go on top. Father had gone back to Adams on business. He had taken Guelma to visit her grandparents. That left Susan to be Mother's chief helper.

Hannah had been on the floor with Daniel, building a house of blocks. As she stood to stretch her legs, she looked out the window. "It's snowing! See, it's snowing!"

Susan dropped her knitting and hurried to join her sister. Snow! At first the big flakes floated down lazily. Then they grew small and came down thick and fast. A real storm had begun.

"I expect," said Susan, "that it's going to snow all night."

"And tomorrow, too, maybe," Hannah added happily. "Look, Susan, let's roast chestnuts to-night."

"And apples," Daniel said.

Susan agreed. "Let's. I can finish my knitting before supper if I keep at it."

"I'll get the table set right away." Hannah left the windows to start laying the plates.

"I'll bring in my chips and kindling." Daniel stood on tiptoe to pull his coat and cap down from the peg by the door.

Susan could never get quite used to having the younger children do her old chores. She wasn't sure she liked it. But she kept on with her knitting until she had rounded off the stock-

110

ing heel. Then she put it in her workbasket and started to help Mother with the supper.

A SNOWY EVENING

Susan was setting the coffeepot on a little three-legged stand over the hot coals when there came a loud stamping at the side door. She opened it to let in Eph, with a swirl of snow-flakes and cold air.

Eph was the hired boy at Father's store. Sometimes he did odd jobs at the mill, too. Now, while Father was away, he was doing the milking and taking care of the horses and the cow for Mother.

He put the pail of milk on the kitchen table. "The snow is certainly falling fast," he said. "I shouldn't wonder if it would be knee-deep by morning. Well, you don't need to fret. Everything is all right down at the barn and the wood-shed is chock-full. I'll be back in the morning.

"Thank you kindly," he added as Mother held toward him a plate of hot gingerbread she had just taken from the oven. With mouth full and hands full he went out into the night.

The children roasted apples and chestnuts as they had planned. They told stories as they sat in front of the fire. Mother told how Grandfather Read had gone off to fight in the Revolu-

tion. Susan told about the Cheshire Cheese. It was still one of her favorite stories.

It should have been a very happy evening. The younger children thought it was. But Susan, suddenly big girl again, felt that Mother wasn't well. It worried her. "Are you sure you feel all right?" she asked anxiously.

"Of course," said Mother. "I'm just tired. That's all."

"You're tired all the time." Susan tried so hard not to sound anxious that she sounded cross instead.

"I'm afraid you are right. But a good night's sleep will help. Now get ready for bed, all of you. It is late."

WHERE IS EPH?

Susan usually slept like a log until Mother called her in the morning. But this morning she was wide awake before the dawn was even gray in the east. "Perhaps," she thought, "I worried over Mother in my sleep. Or maybe when the storm stopped, the sudden stillness startled me."

She slipped carefully from under the blankets so that she wouldn't waken Hannah. Then she hurried downstairs. The fire had been banked the night before. It was easy to start it up again.

"I'll fry the bacon and have the coffee on before Mother gets up," she said to herself. "Maybe I can have the whole breakfast ready. It would be a big help to Mother."

She almost did. Mother was astonished when she came down the four steps that led from her own room. She said she was rested, but Susan thought she didn't look quite like herself.

Having breakfast already fixed upset their usual order of doing things. That was why neither Susan nor Mother noticed at first that Eph hadn't brought in the milk. It wasn't until

Susan started to fill the pitcher that she noticed the bucket wasn't there.

"Mother! What has happened to Eph?"

"He's probably having some trouble getting through the snow. I hope he will be here soon, though. It's long after milking time and feeding time, too."

The family ate their breakfast. Mother started the smaller children on their morning tasks. There was still no sign of Eph. By now the sun had risen. It shone over a world so sparklingly beautiful that Susan caught her breath.

But Mother's thoughts were on the animals out in the stable. "It isn't right to let them suffer. I'll have to go out and take care of them myself."

"You can't," said Susan. "Look, the snow is piled nearly a foot deep against the well curb. It will wear you out to plunge through it."

"I'll put on your father's boots."

"You'll stay right here," said Susan firmly,

115

"until Daniel and I dig a path. It won't hurt the horses or the cow to wait another hour."

Daniel was amazed to hear Susan tell Mother what to do. Susan was surprised herself. She was still more surprised when Mother said meekly, "Well, maybe that would be a good idea."

BREAKING PATHS

Susan hurried into her heaviest coat. She put on long stockings over her shoes to keep the snow from getting in. She found a shovel in the woodshed for herself. Daniel could use the light one with which they took up ashes.

It was hard to push the door open. The snow was banked against it. But once outside she threw back her head to drink in the clean, cold air. The dazzling whiteness everywhere nearly blinded her. "It's a shame to spoil it with shovels," she thought.

But Mother was waiting. Susan and Daniel began to dig with a will. The snow was still light. It hadn't had time to become packed down.

"You look like a storm yourself," Daniel said, "the way you make the snow fly."

Susan was soon warm to her toe tips. Her cheeks glowed. She was almost sorry when she reached the barn door.

Mother had been watching. By the time Susan had opened the door she was coming down the path.

The horses neighed when they went in, as if to say, "What makes you so late?" Old Betsy, the cow, mooed reproachfully.

"But we got here, didn't we?" asked Daniel.

THAT OTHERS MAY FOLLOW

Daniel was old enough to be of real help. Among the three of them the barn work was soon finished. They went back to the house, walking carefully in single file along the newly made path. Susan hated to go in. It would be hard to settle down to pesky indoor chores again. Maybe Mother guessed as much.

"If you aren't too tired, it might be a good idea for you to break a path to the pump and one to the gate," said Mother after the chores in the barn were finished.

Daniel and Susan grabbed up their shovels. They were off again.

They had almost reached the gate when Daniel gave a shout. "Look! There come the men clearing the road!"

Sure enough, down the road came men and oxen. They were breaking away the drifts.

One of the young men dropped back when they reached Susan's gate. It was Aaron McLean. "Here, give me that shovel," he said. "I'll finish your path in a jiffy."

Susan didn't want the path finished in a jiffy, but she knew it wouldn't be polite to say so.

"Eph's mother called to us when we passed her house," Aaron said as he worked. "She asked me to stop here long enough to tell your mother that Eph fell down the cellar steps last night, and got so bruised he can't walk at all today."

"So that's why he didn't get here this morning," thought Susan.

"He was taking care of us, too, while Father is away," said Daniel.

"I didn't know that your father had gone yet. Why, I could have come over the first thing this morning."

"You didn't need to. We've taken care of everything ourselves."

She looked back proudly at her path. Mother had come from the kitchen again and was on her way to the barn with her egg basket.

"You know," said Susan suddenly, "it gives

me a comfortable feeling when I clear paths for other people to use."

Aaron nodded. "I guess," he said after a little while, "the Pilgrim Fathers must have felt something like that when they cleared the way for a new nation in a new country."

"And our great-grandfathers must have felt that way when they settled here."

"Um-hum." Then Aaron grinned. "But I hope their paths weren't so crooked as yours is. It looks like a humpbacked snake."

"Aaron McLean!" Susan scooped up a handful of snow and threw it at him. Aaron dropped the shovel to pick up some snow himself. Daniel joined in. The path-breaking ended in a snowball battle.

How the make-believe cannon balls flew between the "enemy" lines!

"Whew!" cried Aaron at last. "You can throw straighter than you can shovel." He ducked as

Susan tossed a final ball. "I'd better be getting along with the men again."

As he hurried down the road he called back, "Tell your mother not to worry about the outside chores tonight. I'll take care of them. I want to see if I can walk that path of yours without tying myself into a bowknot!"

Ten More Dinners

MOTHER seemed better. She said she was well again. Susan didn't stop worrying about her, though, until Father and Guelma came home. Then a new excitement made her forget everything else. At last Father was going to start their new house.

Night after night, when the supper table had been cleared, he got out his papers and his plans. The children would crowd around him. It was almost as if he were telling them a fairy story about themselves. Two and a half stories high! Fifteen rooms! What would they ever do with so much space?

"Will all of these rooms on the second floor be bedrooms?" Hannah asked.

"Not all of them," said Father. He pointed with his pencil to a square on the plans. "We'll save this big room for something special."

"What?" Guelma asked.

"We'll have a school of our own there."

"Just us?" Susan wanted to know.

"No. We'll ask some of our friends to send their children, too."

Susan thought that over. It would be good to have school right in the house. Then the little children wouldn't have to miss school in bad weather. And if Father picked the teacher himself, she'd be a good one. She wouldn't favor boys over girls. But school at home would keep her from getting outdoors in sunny weather as well as in storms. The walk up and down hill and the games on the way had been the best part of school for Susan.

But there was no need to worry about it just yet. New houses, as the children soon learned, didn't just spring up out of the ground, like dandelions, in a few weeks.

"It will be at least a year before we can move in," their father told them. "First the bricks must be made. And the brickmakers must have a place to board while they work. Do you suppose we can put them up, Mother?"

"How many?" asked Susan.

"Ten or twelve, probably."

"We'll manage," Mother said.

But Susan saw how white she looked. "I wonder," she thought, "if the new house is worth it."

She wondered still more as the time grew near for the men to come. Ten of them to cook for and clean up after! It wasn't strange that Mother looked more and more tired every day.

"See how ill Mother is," Susan told Guelma. "We must do more of her work."

IT SOUNDS EASY

Then, just before the brickmakers arrived in the spring, Baby Eliza was born. She was a precious baby. Susan loved her from the minute Mother let her cuddle the little bundle in her arms. But Susan knew that even the most precious of babies is a lot of work. She could remember when Mary was a baby, and Daniel before her.

"I suppose I was probably a good deal of work

126

myself," she thought. "But no one had to take care of me and ten brickmakers at the same time. I just don't see how Mother can manage it."

Mother couldn't. Her tiredness seemed to get worse and worse. She couldn't even get out of bed. Susan was badly frightened. But the old doctor whom Father called in was cheerful.

"She isn't in any danger," he said. "She is just tired out. Two weeks in bed will do wonders for her. Eph's mother can come take care of her and the baby. Three big girls like you can manage everything else, can't you?"

He made it sound easy. Probably he believed it was. But after he had gone and the three girls were alone, they looked at one another anxiously. Father would have to ask the brickmakers to wait. They were sure of that.

"And then our house won't be built for another year," Guelma said. "All of us will be old women before we move in."

"Maybe," Susan said thoughtfully, "the doctor is right. After all, we do know how to do nearly everything Mother does. And it isn't as if she were miles away. It's just four steps up to her room from the kitchen. We can ask her what to do if we don't know. And we can show her everything we cook before we give it to the men. You know, it might be fun—doing things ourselves instead of just helping her to do them."

"That's right," Guelma agreed.

"What shall we start on?" asked Hannah.

"Mother will tell us," Susan said.

When they peeped in at her door, she was asleep. They tiptoed down to the kitchen. There they looked anxiously at one another again.

"Bread," said Susan positively. "That's one thing we'll always need. And it's one thing we know how to make."

The girls started in on bread.

Soon they were too busy to be anxious.

128

The brickmakers began their work the next morning. The ten pails for their dinners were lined up in a row on the kitchen table.

The girls had begun even before the brickmakers. "Twenty loaves of bread," said Susan. "That ought to give us a good start. And cheese —we must cut the slices good and thick."

"Shall we start the gingerbread now?" Hannah asked.

"You mix it," Guelma told her, "while I get the oven heated."

By noon the dinner pails were neatly packed.

"They smell fine," said Hannah.

"I hope the men will think so, too."

"They will if they're hungry enough," Susan said tartly. "And men generally are hungry."

She herself thought the pails looked pretty good. "Maybe, though, we'd better see what Mother says about them."

130

They tiptoed carefully up the stairs to Mother's room. Already she seemed stronger. She peeped into each pail as the girls lifted the cover. "That one is good. The crust on this gingerbread is a little burned. You'd better put in another slice."

After she had looked at the last one, she leaned back against her pillows. "You've done very well," she said quietly.

The girls filed back down the steps. They put the dinner pails on the side porch. Daniel could take them down to the men.

"And now," said Guelma, "I suppose we'll have to start getting supper under way."

"Wait a minute," Susan told her. "There's something important that comes first."

"What, for goodness sake?"

"We have forgotten something. Can you guess?" asked Susan as she sat down wearily.

"No, I can't guess." Guelma looked and looked about the kitchen for the forgotten thing.

"Us. We've forgotten to make any dinner for ourselves."

They looked at one another. Then they began to laugh. It wasn't specially funny to forget your own dinner. But they had proved to themselves what they could do. Mother was pleased. The brickmaking was started. Somehow, it just seemed to be a good time to laugh.

Wishes

THE DOCTOR was right. After two weeks' rest Mother could move around in her room. In two weeks more she was able to take care of her family again.

Of course Susan was pleased, but she felt let down, too. She'd been doing things her own way. It was hard to go back to following someone else's plans, even when that someone else was Mother.

"I wish something exciting would happen."

"Would it be exciting to drive me out to Friend Inge's this afternoon?" Mother asked. "I want to see if he can let me have some potatoes."

Susan shook her head. "Not the least bit exciting," she said honestly. "But I'll be glad to do it, if you aren't strong enough yet to take the reins."

It was a pleasant afternoon. On the way out Susan and Mother stopped at the place where the new house would be. On the way back they went to the store.

When Susan was little she'd thought Father's store was mysterious and exciting. Today she felt that it was dull. "It's filled with things that I either don't want or can't have. Now if I had some money of my own——"

Mother was looking at a set of blue cups and saucers which had just been unpacked. "See, Susan," she said softly. "Aren't they beautiful? Oh, how I wish I could have them!"

Susan was startled. She had never known before that Mother longed for pretty things. "Why don't you ask Father for them?"

Mother shook her head. "Every penny has to go into the new house." She gave the china a last loving look, then turned to Eph. "I want you to bring me a new water bucket."

"Look, Mother," Susan said as they left the store. "There comes the first load of hay I've seen this year. Abby says if you wish on a load of hay and then don't see it again, your wish will come true. Quick! Wish before it turns the corner!"

Mother laughed. "Susan Anthony! Aren't you ever going to start growing up?"

"Well, it doesn't do any harm to wish. There! I've made mine."

"I suppose you wished for something exciting to happen."

"M-m-m," said Susan. "It might be bad luck to tell. I suppose *you* wished for the blue china?"

"Do you think I wished?" laughed Mother.

"Yes, I think you did," Susan answered.

"M-m-m," teased Mother. "Don't you wish you knew?" She smiled sweetly.

A SPOOLER IS NEEDED

Father seemed worried that evening. Something must have gone wrong at the mill.

136

"Did a machine break down?" asked Hannah.

"No, but one of our best spoolers had to go home sick, and there is no one to take her place."

"Let me!" cried Susan. Why, this was the exciting thing she had been wishing for!

But Guelma was eager, too. "Let me! I'm older. Susan is too young for millwork."

"There are girls there younger than either of you. They work twelve hours a day just as the grown women do," put in Father.

"It's nonsense for either of you to think of it," Mother told them. "Millwork is for girls who have to earn their own bread. So long as you have a father to take care of you——"

"They may not have me always," Father interrupted.

"Then they will have a husband or a brother."

"Maybe," Father said thoughtfully. "But it might not be a bad idea for them to learn what earning their own living feels like."

"Well, we don't have to decide it this minute. Suppose you dish up supper, girls, while I finish my darning."

Guelma whispered to Susan as they bent over the fireplace, "That means she and Father will talk it over after they are alone."

"Mother will give in. She always does," Susan whispered back hopefully.

"But which one of us will they let do it?"

"I hate to disappoint you, my dear sister, but I wished on a load of hay this afternoon that something would happen to me. So I'm sure to be the one." Susan began to giggle at her own nonsense.

Guelma opened the little Dutch oven. "I hate to disappoint you, my dear sister," she said, giggling back, "but I wished on the first star this evening that I could have a beaded bag, like Abby's sister's. And the only way I'll ever get one is to earn it myself."

138

"It seems, then," said Susan, "to be a fight between haycart and star."

DRAWING STRAWS

Susan had never been good at waiting. She could hardly sleep that night. Mother didn't need to hurry her the next morning, either. Guelma was excited, too. Both of them were downstairs by the time Mother finished calling.

It wasn't until after family prayers, though, that Mother said quietly, "We have decided, girls, that it will be good training for one of you to work a few days in the mill. We wish we could let you both do it, but even if there were work for two, I could spare only one. Whoever stays home will have double duty here. That means that the sister who goes should divide her wages with the sister who stays."

"Of course," said the girls together.

"Then maybe you had better draw straws to see who goes with Father this morning."

Father took a piece of woolen thread from Mother's workbasket. He cut it into a long and a short piece. "Long piece goes to the mill. Short piece stays home," he announced. He put his hands behind his back and turned to Guelma. "Which hand do you choose?"

"—I—I choose the right hand," Guelma stuttered, she was so excited.

Father opened the right hand. It held the short piece.

Guelma's face was long for a minute, but she was a good loser. She managed to smile as she turned to Susan. "Haycart won. I'll pack your dinner pail while you get ready to go."

Susan, the Millworker

SUSAN had been inside the mill only a few times. Father never liked to have anyone, not even his own family, go through the great gates except on business. Susan was on business now. Her heart beat rapidly as she and Father drew near to the long building.

"I'm not afraid," she told herself sternly. "Of course I'm not afraid. I'm just excited."

They waited at the gates for a big wagon piled high with boxes to come through. Then they crossed to the door of the first room. The clatter inside made Susan's head swim. Everything was moving and everything was noisy. There were pulleys and belts and spindles. There were whirring and buzzing and clashing. Over it all hung the smell of oily machinery. The great spinning frames made the girls who worked by them look like tiny things.

"But they aren't," Susan told herself. "It's just the opposite. The frames are captive giants who must obey them."

The foreman was bending over a machine on the far side of the room. He hardly looked up when Father led Susan over to him.

"Here is a girl to hold Mary's place for her until she can come back," Father said.

"Good," said the foreman. "I'll take care of her in a minute. The foreman in the weaving room wants you to come over there as soon as you can. There's some trouble——"

"I shall go immediately."

Father was gone without even a good-by. Susan realized that she was on her own now.

The foreman straightened up. He wiped an oily hand across his forehead. It left an oily smear.

"Myra!" he called.

Susan didn't see how anyone could hear him above the clatter of the machinery. But a girl about her own age came hurrying from the other end of the room.

"Here is the new girl to take Mary's place. You can show her what to do." The foreman followed Father toward the weaving room.

Myra looked at Susan. "If you're as scared as I was my first day, your knees are knocking each other black and blue this very minute. But there's nothing to be afraid of, really. The machines won't bite you—unless you get too close. And you won't have to work nearly so hard here as you do at home. I know I don't."

"What do I have to do?" asked Susan.

"You're a spooler. I'm one, too. We have to

change the spools, or bobbins, on the frames. Take them off when they are full and put on empty ones. See!"

Myra showed Susan the correct way to remove a spool of bright-colored thread. Quickly an empty spool must be put in its place to wind up the new thread as the huge machine spun it.

Susan followed her from frame to frame as she collected the bobbins filled with spun thread and slipped empty ones into their places.

"There! That's all for a while," Myra said. "It takes a good half hour for the spools to wind themselves full. Come meet the other girls."

Some of them Susan already knew. They came to the village school during the winter and worked in the mill during the summer. But there still were more girls to get acquainted with than she had ever met at one time.

She liked to meet people. Soon her heart left her throat and went back where it belonged. By

the time the whistle blew that evening, she felt as if she had been a millhand for weeks.

REASONS FOR WORKING

The next two weeks were the busiest she had ever known. Her working day was long. It began at six in the morning and ended at six at night. The work itself wasn't hard, but it wasn't any lazy girl's dream, either. She was sure she walked miles every day, up and down between the spinning frames.

While they waited for the spools to fill, she and Myra could play games over in one corner of the big room. Sometimes, too, the foreman would let them visit the other parts of the mill where the cotton was combed into rolls or where the weaving was done. Once he even let them go down into the cellar, where they could peep through the door at the big water wheel.

Best of all, Susan liked to visit with the other girls and listen to them talk.

"I enjoy it," she said to Myra. "Every one of them has a different reason for leaving home to come to work. Bess wants to get money to buy her wedding clothes. Jenny has a sick mother. Faith is saving everything to send her brother to college. What do you do with your money, Myra?"

"Nothing. Father comes to town on payday and takes every cent of it."

"How can he? You earned it. It's your money."

Myra shook her head. "The law says everything a child earns belongs to his father. I wouldn't mind if Mother could just have part of it, too—just enough for her to get a decent dress. But she can't. It all belongs to Father, and he keeps it. Every penny!" Myra glared at Susan almost as if she were to blame.

147

"I was glad when the foreman called me to run an errand," Susan told Guelma that evening. "I didn't know what to say. But just saying things won't help much. Somebody ought to do something."

She put her prettiest handkerchief in her pocket the next morning to take to the mill. She slipped it into Myra's hand. "Give this to your mother," she said.

One little handkerchief didn't help much, and she knew it. But it did help a little.

WISHES COME TRUE

Mary came back to work in two weeks. Susan was glad, of course, that Mary was well again. But she was very far from glad that her own work in the mill was over. She would have been downright blue except for one thing. The most thrilling part of the two weeks was still to come.

148

That last evening, when she left, the foreman gave her her wages.

Three dollars for two weeks' work! She felt very wealthy as she carried it home.

Half of it belonged to Guelma. And Guelma knew exactly what she was going to do with it.

She hurried down to the village the next morning. When she came back she had a beaded bag. It was so beautiful it almost took Susan's breath. She was as delighted as Guelma. They turned the bag this way and that in the sunlight to make the beads flash and sparkle.

"You see," Guelma said happily, "my wish on the star came true, after all."

"What are you going to do with your money?" Hannah asked Susan. "Have you made up your mind yet?"

"I made it up even before I started to work. What's more, I bought it on my way home last night." She went out into the hall and came back with a box which she put in front of Mother. "For me?" asked Mother, surprised. "But it's not my birthday."

"This is just an everyday present."

Mother opened the box. Inside, carefully packed in straw, were the blue cups and saucers.

Mother was delighted. "But you shouldn't have spent all your money on me."

"I had to. If your wish hadn't come true as well as mine, Guelma could say there was something wrong with our haycart!"

The New Home

IT TOOK a long time to build the new house. Susan was thirteen years old before the last workmen packed their tools and left.

Then the cleaning began. Windows were washed. Floors were polished. Back at the old house, too, there was plenty of work to be done. Carpets had to be taken up and curtains taken down. Dishes and books had to be packed.

"We're in such a rush," Susan told Hannah, "I have to draw my breath twice at once."

But she always had time to show the new house to friends when they came by. "Everyone likes to go through a new house," she explained.

"And maybe you like to show it off a bit, too," her brother teased.

On her way home from meeting the Sunday before the furniture was to be moved, she met Myra. Myra still worked twelve hours a day in the mill. They didn't see much of each other. They stopped now for a few minutes' chat.

Myra looked up at the new house. "It is a fine place," she said. "I've never seen one so grand."

"Would you like to go through it?" Susan asked eagerly.

"That I would." Myra was eager, too.

"Come along, then."

Susan opened the door. The house, of course, was empty. But it was beautiful. The living-room walls were of hard plaster. The woodwork was tinted light green.

"And Mother has some new chairs painted black with rush bottoms. Won't they look fine against the green woodwork?"

Myra agreed. "This would be a wonderful place to have a party."

"Wouldn't it? Of course we couldn't have any dancing, but we could have a party with games. I'll ask Mother."

Myra didn't like the upstairs rooms so well as she did the first floor. When they came to the big new schoolroom she made a face at it.

"But it's just as fine a room as those downstairs," Susan told her. "And Father is going to have a stool for each of the children so that they won't be crowded together on one bench. There will be schoolbooks with pictures in them, too!"

Myra only laughed. "You can't change my mind. I like parties. I hate school."

FROM PARTY TO SCHOOL

The next day the moving began. Then, as soon as they were settled, Father wrote to one

153

of his cousins, Sarah Anthony. He invited her to teach in their new home school. Cousin Sarah agreed to come.

For the next several months Susan had no time to think of the party she had talked about with Myra. When she did get around to it, though, Mother was willing.

"And may I ask Myra?"

"Of course."

"There's something else I'd like to do for her, only I don't know how to go about it."

"What is that?"

"I'd like to show her that all schools aren't like the terrible one she went to. She used to tell me about it. It didn't have any windows. It didn't have any desks. There was just a board nailed to the wall for the children to write on. And the schoolmaster spent almost as much time whipping the children as he did teaching them. She hates school, and I don't blame her."

"Neither do I," Mother agreed.

"Besides, even if she wanted to go back to such a horrid old place, she couldn't because she has to work all day. It's just too bad. She's bright as a button, and she needs more schooling. Why, she can't read anything but little words!"

"She isn't the only worker in the mills who needs more schooling," Father said. "I've been thinking about it for quite a while. We've already started a night class for men. But the girls should have a chance, too. I've been wondering. Suppose we started a school for them in our own schoolroom on Sunday afternoons. What would you think of that, Cousin Sarah?"

"I'll be glad to teach them if Susan and Guelma will help."

"I'll invite Myra to the party and to the school at the same time," Susan said.

Susan invited Myra that very day.

"I don't care for school," said Myra.

"You'll enjoy it," Susan insisted. "Come just once, anyway, and see what it's like."

Myra wouldn't promise. "I'll think about it."

Abby had been listening to the talk between Susan and Myra. Now she lost patience. "Let the girl alone, Susan. You can't help a person who doesn't want to be helped."

"I can so," Susan insisted, "if I just go about it in the right way. Only I don't seem to know which way is right."

THE PARTY

The night of the party was clear and cold. After the guests had taken off their heavy coats in the hallway, they crowded around the fireplace. At first they were shy, but their shyness thawed away as they grew warm. Soon they were romping all over the house.

Susan hadn't expected such a boisterous

crowd. She hardly knew what to do. She tried
to get them to play quiet games, but that wasn't
much better. When they sat down they pushed
their chairs back against the wall. Most of the

boys had slicked their hair with oil. It left a smear where their heads touched the plaster. Their hobnailed boots nicked the woodwork.

All of her guests were having a good time. There was no doubt about that. Susan tried to have a good time with them. But her eyes kept going to the smeared plaster and scarred woodwork. Mother had worked so hard to make the room just right. So had they all. And now it was almost ruined. She wanted to cry.

Myra knew how she felt. "Don't worry," she whispered. "Most of it will wash off. I know it will."

"Even if it does wash off, Mother will be sad when she sees it tomorrow," said Susan.

"She won't have to see it this way. After the party, I'll help clean the room," offered Myra.

Susan was still downcast. She had been a good friend to Myra. Myra wanted to be a good friend to her. She could think of only one way, now, to cheer Susan up. As she left she whispered, "Look, Susan. I'll come to your school next Sunday. Honest I will."

SCHOOL IS A SUCCESS

Myra kept her word. On Sunday afternoon she was the first of the mill girls to arrive. She was as surprised as Susan expected her to be when she saw the cheerful schoolroom, with its separate seat for each student. She was delighted with the picture books, too.

"I'll get things started," Cousin Sarah told Susan, "but I've promised to help nurse old Mrs. Simpson this afternoon. You'll have to take charge of things after I leave."

Susan nodded. She was a little frightened after Cousin Sarah left, but she did her best. And her best was very good. The girls were so interested they didn't want to leave when school was over.

159

Myra had been the first to come. Now she was the last to go. She kept looking at Susan with a puzzled frown. "Remember what I told you last summer? I liked parties and I hated school. Now you've got me all mixed up. You've made me hate parties and like school. Honestly, Susan, you're the most upsetting girl I ever met."

Susan,
the Teacher

AT FIRST Susan taught only in the Sunday school. Soon, though, she began to help Cousin Sarah on weekdays, too. Then she and Guelma taught the home school during the summer by themselves. The next winter Susan helped some friends start a home school like Cousin Sarah's.

But none of this made her feel the least bit like a teacher. She was just Big Sister, helping the younger children with their lessons. It was a surprise when the school board in a near-by town asked her to teach for the summer term.

"My goodness gracious," she told her father, "I thought you had to be at least eighteen years old before you could become a teacher! I'm nowhere near that yet. What put such an idea into their heads?"

"It isn't a bad one. You have had a good deal more schooling than many a teacher who is eighteen or over. And the experience might do you good. Every girl should have experience in earning her own living. Then, if ever she has to do it, she will be ready.

"Besides," he added with a smile, "nothing makes a person appreciate home so much as getting away from it for a while."

Susan looked around their comfortable kitchen. It was so clean that it sparkled. "I don't have to go away to love it."

After she thought it over, though, she decided Father was right. "I'll get a chance to see how other people live," she told Abby. "The teacher, you know, has to 'board around.' I'll stay in a different home each week."

"Humph!" said Abby. "You won't have time to unpack before you're packing up again."

"It will be fun, anyway."

"And how will you know what to teach the children?"

"I'll teach them anything they want to learn. If any of *my* girl pupils want long division, they are going to get it!"

ON HER OWN

She wasn't quite so sure of herself when Father left her and her small trunk at the first home where she was to stay. The sun blazed down into the room she was to share with the girls of the house. Her hands felt cold as she smoothed her hair before the tiny mirror. A schoolteacher, of course, couldn't wear her braids little-girl fashion, hanging down her back. Still, it seemed strange to have them pinned up firmly.

163

It seemed still more strange at the supper table to be talking with the grown people instead of keeping quiet with the children. After supper it was rather nice to sit with her crocheting while the children washed the dishes. But later, when the children ran around the yard in a wild game of tag, it wasn't so much fun to stay quietly with the older folk.

Schoolteachers mustn't be afraid, she kept telling herself the next morning as she opened the schoolhouse. But there was no harm in being excited. That was all she was—just excited.

She put her books and her ruler on the big desk. She took off her bonnet. Then she picked up the ruler again and went to the entryway. There she rapped her ruler sharply against the door to call the children in.

As they came running up they reminded her of chickens when she scattered feed. "Goodness!" she thought. "There must be hundreds."

But after she got them seated and had taken their names, she found there were only thirty. Very few big boys came to school during the summer. They were all at work in the fields. Susan couldn't help being glad for that.

"Now," she said briskly after she had taken the roll. "Let me see your schoolbooks. I must know what your parents want you to study."

One by one the children came to her desk to show their schoolbooks. No two were alike. Some had the spellers their mothers had used when they were little. Some had readers that had belonged to their big brothers. One child had a new book. She had put a cover over it very carefully to hide its newness.

The last little girl had no book at all.

"Why, Eliza Jones," Susan said, "did you stop to play on the way to school and lose your book?"

Eliza shook her head very positively. "I didn't lose it. I haven't got any. Ma says it isn't any use for me to learn to read and spell. If you'll teach me to sew, that's all she wants. You can sew real pretty. Cousin Mamie saw a sampler you made——"

"Of course I'll teach you to sew," Susan said. "But you must learn to read, too."

"But Ma says——"

"I'll go see your mother this afternoon."

MORE THAN ONE CAN BE STUBBORN

The older girls stayed to help Susan clean the school that afternoon. They hadn't known what a worker she was. It took their breath away to keep up with her.

"There!" said one of them at last. "The place is so clean you can smell it. But, good lands, you must be worn to a frazzle!"

Susan was tired, but she had one more task to do before the long day was over. She must go to see Eliza Jones's mother. As she put on her bonnet, her face wore what Daniel called "Sister's do-or-die look."

Mrs. Jones's face took on very much the same expression when Susan explained her errand. "There isn't a speck of use in your teaching my Eliza reading and spelling and such things that she will never use. Just you give her a good stiff stint of sewing and see that she keeps at it."

"But every girl should learn how to read."

"Eliza knows her letters and she can spell easy words. I guess that's enough."

"It isn't," Susan insisted.

"I know how to raise my own child."

"Oh, dear!" Susan thought. "What makes her so stubborn?" Then a new idea came into her head. "Why, maybe that's exactly what she's thinking about me. All right, I *am* stubborn. But at least I can be polite about it."

She began again. "Of course you know best.

It *is* important for Eliza to learn to sew. But it's important for her to learn to read and write, too. And there's no reason whatever why she can't do both."

Mrs. Jones looked doubtful.

"I tell you what we'll do," Susan went on: "I'll fix a sampler for her, and let her work on it mornings. But you get her a speller and she can study that in the afternoons."

Mrs. Jones still looked doubtful. But Daniel could have told her that when his sister had on her do-or-die look, she usually got what she wanted. When Susan left, Mrs. Jones had agreed that Eliza could learn to read and write and spell.

EXHIBITION DAY

It seemed to Susan that the twelve weeks were over almost before they were started. In almost no time she and the children were getting ready

169

for Exhibition Day. It would be the last day of school.

The last morning was filled with hustle and bustle. The girls brought flowers to trim the room. They scrubbed and polished until everything sparkled almost as brightly as Mother's kitchen in Battenville.

All the while they worked, everyone was asking everyone else to hear her say her piece over one last time. Susan was as excited as any of them. It was her Exhibition Day, too.

The children's parents came in the afternoon. Some of them sat on the back benches. Others stood against the walls. The little schoolhouse was packed.

Susan passed around samples of her pupils' writing. She showed aprons the children had made and samples on which they were working.

"They've done right well," the mothers told one another.

Then the closing exercises began. Some of the children read their own compositions. Others read or recited poems from their readers. Susan was most pleased when Eliza read a whole poem without a single mistake.

"There now!" Mrs. Jones told her neighbor. "Eliza is a smart child, if I do say so myself.

171

And the teacher is right. It doesn't do Eliza a mite of harm to read and write, even if she is a girl-child."

"Teacher is a bit young," the neighbor agreed, "but she has a good headpiece on her."

Father had driven over to take Susan home. He came into the schoolroom just in time to hear the women talking. He looked over their heads to where Susan sat at her desk, and smiled at her. Susan heard them, too. She smiled back. It would have been hard to say who was happier.

The Mill
Closes Down

Susan was glad the drive home was a long one. It gave her a chance to talk with Father. Usually he was too busy for long talks.

"I want to go back to school," she told him. "Teaching has taught me how much I still need to know."

Father nodded. "That probably is a wise thing for you to do. Maybe I can send both you and Guelma to Deborah Moulson's school, down in Pennsylvania, this winter."

Susan was half pleased, half frightened. Pennsylvania was a long way from home.

She told Abby about it the next day while they

173

went down to the store on an errand. Abby didn't like the idea at all.

"It's nonsense! And you've done enough silly things already, Susan. You taught school when you didn't have to. That was enough to get you talked about. I've heard several women say no girl can go out of her home to work like that and still be a lady."

"Thank goodness Father doesn't feel that way!" Susan told her. "He says girls have just as much right to earn their living as boys do. It's their duty to learn how. I think so, too."

"Not when they have a father to support them. And now you talk about going back to school, when goodness knows you have too much education already!"

They were still arguing when they reached the store. Susan only half heard what the men around the stove were talking about. It wasn't until months later that she remembered.

"It's President Jackson's fault!" one of them was almost shouting. "If he hadn't closed down the United States Bank, the country wouldn't be in such a fix. We've got hard times ahead of us now, and no mistake!"

"You're right," another man said. "I shouldn't be surprised if a hundred years from now, history books were still telling about 'The Panic of 1837.'"

"Things go around in a circle," the first man said. "Thousands of people are out of work. They haven't any money to buy anything. Without customers, the stores are beginning to fail. Without stores to buy their goods, factories and mills will have to close down. That will put thousands more people out of work. And then it starts all over again!"

"Just like my arguments with Abby," Susan thought. "Around and around!"

SAD NEWS

During her first months at Deborah Moulson's school there were times when Susan felt as if Abby might have been right. Maybe it was silly for her to go back to school. She was home-sick, very homesick. It was hard to be a pupil again after she had been a teacher. And she was sure she had never scolded her scholars half so sharply as the headmistress scolded her.

Susan had common sense, though. Whenever she found herself thinking such thoughts she would work harder than ever. "As long as I'm here, I might as well get all the education I possibly can."

Father had planned to come for Guelma and Susan when school closed in the spring. Instead, he sent a letter. Would they be afraid to come home alone if he couldn't get there?

Susan was worried. "Of course we wouldn't be afraid," she said to Guelma. "I think it would be exciting to travel by ourselves. But why can't he come? Is something wrong?"

Uneasily, then, she remembered what the men at the store had said about mills closing down.

But not Father's mill! Oh, surely, not Father's great mill!

She was relieved when a week later he wrote again. He was going to Washington on business and could come for them, after all, on his way home.

"This," she told Guelma, "must mean that whatever was wrong is all straightened out now."

BAD NEWS

But it didn't. She knew that as soon as she got a good look at Father. He seemed years older. His face was filled with worry lines.

At first he talked cheerfully enough. He told them how he had ridden on the railroad cars all the way from Baltimore to Washington. "It was nearly forty miles, and it took only two hours."

Susan was delighted. "Some day I'll ride on them myself."

178

"You'll like it," he told her, "but only if you can have a good wash-up as soon as you get off the cars. You'll be so covered with soot and cinders your own mother wouldn't know you." He laughed, but then his face sank back quickly into its worry lines again.

"What's the matter, Father?" Guelma asked. "Is Mother ill?"

"No," he answered. Then he said quietly, "I've closed down the mill."

Closed down the mill! Susan wouldn't let herself believe it. The big dripping mill wheel couldn't have stopped! The whir and clatter of the great spinning frames couldn't have become still! The busy girls——

"What will become of the workers?" she asked.

"They will suffer cruelly. It was for their sake I tried to keep things going, even after there was no market for the goods they made. But now

I've come to the end of my rope. I've lost every-thing—mill, store, our home and our furniture."

Susan put her hand on his arm. "You haven't lost us," she reminded him. "And you've trained us to support ourselves. We'll start looking for schools to teach just as soon as we get home."

"It would be well to visit with your mother just a few days first," Father told her. He smiled as he said it. When he smiled he didn't look quite so old and weary.

IT WILL NEVER BE HOME AGAIN

Susan was glad to be home again, even though she knew it would soon be home no longer. No one had time to stop and worry over troubles. There was too much to be done. Lists must be made of the things to be sold.

Father wouldn't hold anything out. "I must pay every penny I owe," he said.

180

Their precious books were on the list. So were Father's spectacles and even the boys' knives.

The house must be shown to would-be buyers. The garden must be kept up. Canning food to be used next winter was more important than ever now.

Susan knew that if she stayed home there would be something for her to do every minute of the day. But she knew, too, that Mary and Hannah were no longer little children. They could help Mother now as much as she and Guelma ever had.

Guelma could stay home a little longer to make sure they knew how, but the sooner Susan started teaching, the better.

Schools were opening for the summer term. She had received a good offer. "I'll come," she wrote to the school board.

It didn't take long to pack her trunk. Her best petticoats, her good shawl, her net gloves had all been put in with the things to sell. She could take only what she had to have.

Out in the kitchen Hannah was packing a lunch for her to take with her. Guelma was pressing the dress she would wear tomorrow.

Mother brought in her old bonnet. "I do wish you could have a new one. Still, you always look well in this. I've put on new ribbons.

"Now, you must get to bed, Susan, or you'll be all worn out tomorrow before you start."

Susan shut the lid of her trunk and stood up. "All right. But I need to stretch a little. I'm going out to the pump for a dipper of water."

Outdoors, moonlight was spilling over the whole hillside. Susan got her water. Then she turned for a last look around her.

"It's home tonight," she said to herself, "but it will never be home again." She remembered her excitement when she had gone away to teach before. There were no thrills now. To her surprise

there was something better. It was a warm feeling that she was needed.

"It's good," she thought, "to be able to help my family. I know the neighbors are sorry for me, but they don't need to be. I'm happy."

A Life of Service

FOR SEVERAL years Susan taught and helped her family. Then times grew better. At last her help was no longer needed.

"Now," Abby wrote her, "you can give up your work and settle down at home."

Not Susan! By this time her longing to help others had reached beyond her family. It went out to everyone in need.

At first she worked with groups promoting temperance. Then she joined those who were fighting against slavery. Most of all, she wanted to help the girls and women of America and all over the whole world.

184

There were thousands of girls like Myra who had to work twelve hours a day in factories and mills. Then there were all the girls like Eliza who had no chance to get an education just because they were girls. There were thousands of women whose wages were less than half what men received for the same work. There were all the women who, because they were married, could not own property. Their homes, salaries, and children belonged to their husbands.

Susan wanted to help them all. And she was sure there was only one best way to do it. If women could vote, then they could help themselves. She gave the rest of her long life to getting them this right—the right to vote.

THE WOMAN'S RIGHTS CONVENTION

It wasn't easy at first. Neither men nor women were ready for Susan's ideas.

In 1853 there was a woman's rights convention in New York. The great hall was crowded.

"Look!" said one woman to her neighbor. "There's Susan Anthony on the platform. She has on trousers, just like a man! How awful!"

"They aren't like a man's at all," her neighbor insisted. "They are wide and full. See how she has gathered them in around the ankle. They are a lot more sensible than the long heavy skirts most women wear. She calls them bloomers."

"I don't care what she calls them. They're awful. She ought to be ashamed of herself. And she ought to be ashamed of the nonsense she preaches, too. 'Votes for Women'! It's ridiculous! Woman's place is in the home."

"Be quiet," whispered her neighbor. "She's getting up to speak."

But the angry woman wouldn't be quiet. Neither would many other people in the large crowd. "Sit down!" they cried to Susan.

There were hisses and groans and catcalls. The crowd became a mob. Not even the police could keep them quiet. The meeting broke up.

"There!" said an angry man as the crowd pushed its way out from the building. "She'll never dare keep on with her nonsense now. We won't hear any more from Susan B. Anthony."

AT THE WORLD'S FAIR

He didn't know Susan. Of course she dared. She wasn't stopped at all. People laughed at her. They scoffed at her. They fought against her. She kept on. At last they began, very slowly, to listen to what she had to say.

In 1893 there was a great World's Fair in Chicago. Men and women came from all parts of the world to see its wonders. One building was particularly crowded. Hundreds of people stood outside in line, waiting for a chance to get in.

"What's going on here?" a young girl asked as she joined the line. She was sure it must be something she shouldn't miss.

"It's the World's Congress of Women," an older woman told her. "Susan Anthony is to speak today."

"I've heard my mother talk about her. She's been fighting for woman's rights for forty years. Mother doesn't believe in votes for women, but she says she does believe that Miss Anthony is a fine, brave woman."

"That she is!"

A carriage drove up to the sidewalk. The crowd pushed toward it. Policemen had to make a way for the white-haired woman who was trying to get from the carriage to the building. But this crowd wasn't an angry mob. Far from it!

"Three cheers for Susan Anthony!" someone called. The crowd took it up. They cheered and cheered for this brave woman.

"My, but she must be proud!" said the girl.

The older woman shook her head. "Susan doesn't care the snap of a finger about being popular herself. Now, if the crowd would cheer for 'Votes for Women'——"

"But they will never do that!"

"Not in her lifetime, I'm afraid. She's an old woman. But Susan's ideas will live after her. And the time will come."

VICTORY

The woman was right. Susan died in 1906, but her ideas lived.

On Election Day in 1920, there were long lines in front of every voting booth in the United States. In these lines were women as well as men. At last women could vote!

So many were eager to use this new right that in many places they had to stand in line two or three hours while they waited for their turn. There were housewives and business women, schoolteachers and factory girls. They talked with one another while they waited.

In the city of Rochester, New York, the lines were especially long.

"If only Susan Anthony were alive today," said a white-haired woman, "how happy she would be!"

"Who was Susan Anthony?" asked a factory girl. "I don't believe I've ever heard of her."

"You haven't lived in Rochester very long then."

"No, just a few months."

"I thought so, because everybody in Rochester knows our Susan. She lived here a good many years. It was she who did most to open the University of Rochester to women."

"Why should she be especially happy today?" asked the girl.

"Because she gave you the right to vote."

"I thought the Nineteenth Amendment to the Constitution did that."

"But she was the mother of the Nineteenth Amendment."

"Some people call it the Susan Anthony Amendment," a stenographer said. "There's a monument to her and two of her friends down in Washington. I saw it when I was on my vacation last summer."

"But the real monument to Susan is not made of stone," said the white-haired woman.

"Why not?" the factory girl asked.

"Because it is made of living women like yourself. And it will last as long as they work with the vote she helped them win—work to make the world the better place that she wanted it to be."

"Oh!" said the girl. "Oh!" she said again.

And then it was her turn to vote.